MW01230490

PROTECTING OCEAN ANIMALS

LAUREN KUKLA

Consulting Editor, Diane Craig, M.A./Reading Specialist

Sandcastle

An Imprint of Abdo Publishing
abdopublishing.com

abdopublishing.com

Published by Abdo Publishing, a division of ABDO, PO Box 398166, Minneapolis, Minnesota 55439. Copyright © 2017 by Abdo Consulting Group, Inc. International copyrights reserved in all countries. No part of this book may be reproduced in any form without written permission from the publisher. SandCastle™ is a trademark and logo of Abdo Publishing.

Printed in the United States of America, North Mankato, Minnesota
102016
012017

THIS BOOK CONTAINS
RECYCLED MATERIALS

Editor: Rebecca Felix
Content Developer: Nancy Tuminelly
Cover and Interior Design and Production: Mighty Media, Inc.
Photo Credits: David Doubilet/National Geographic/Getty Images, Shutterstock Images

Publisher's Cataloging-in-Publication Data

Names: Kukla, Lauren, author.
Title: Protecting ocean animals / by Lauren Kukla.
Description: Minneapolis, MN : Abdo Publishing, 2017. | Series: Awesome
   animals in their habitats
Identifiers: LCCN 2016944680 | ISBN 9781680784282 (lib. bdg.) |
   ISBN 9781680797817 (ebook)
Subjects: LCSH: Animals--Habitations--Juvenile literature. | Habitat (Ecology)--
   Juvenile literature. | Wildlife conservation--Juvenile literature.
Classification: DDC 577--dc23
LC record available at http://lccn.loc.gov/2016944680

SandCastle™ Level: Transitional

SandCastle™ books are created by a team of professional educators, reading specialists, and content developers around five essential components—phonemic awareness, phonics, vocabulary, text comprehension, and fluency—to assist young readers as they develop reading skills and strategies and increase their general knowledge. All books are written, reviewed, and leveled for guided reading, early reading intervention, and Accelerated Reader™ programs for use in shared, guided, and independent reading and writing activities to support a balanced approach to literacy instruction. The SandCastle™ series has four levels that correspond to early literacy development. The levels are provided to help teachers and parents select appropriate books for young readers.

EMERGING · BEGINNING · TRANSITIONAL · FLUENT

CONTENTS

ABOUT OCEANS

Oceans are large bodies
of water.

They are filled with salt water. Many animals live in oceans.

Some ocean animals are big.

Whales can be bigger than
school buses!

Other ocean life
is small.

Zooplankton are very small. They are almost too small to see.

Some animals live deep in the ocean. No light can reach here.

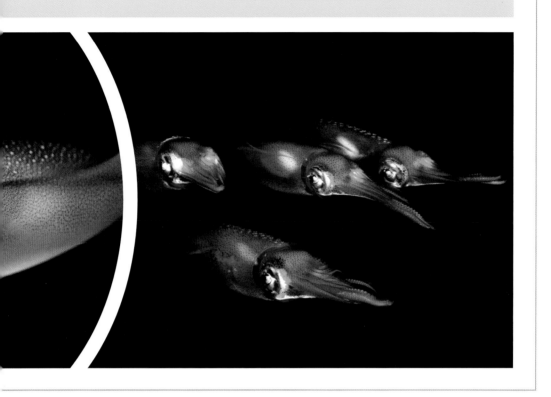

Squid can live in deep water.

Other animals live in **shallow** water. Sunlight shines through the water.

Lots of fish live here.
Dolphins do too.

Coral **reefs** form in some **shallow** water. They are home to many animals.

Sea urchins live there. So do
lobsters.

Sharks hunt in coral **reefs**.

Eugenie Clark was an **oceanographer**. She studied sharks.

Ocean animals are at **risk**. **Pollution** makes the water unsafe for them.

People eat fish from oceans.
Sometimes they take too many of
one kind of fish.

You can help **protect** oceans.

Pick up trash on beaches. Only eat fish that have healthy **populations**.

THINK ABOUT IT

Have you ever visited an ocean?
What animals did you see there?

GLOSSARY

oceanographer – a person who studies the ocean and its plants and animals.

pollution – contamination of the air, water, or soil caused by man-made waste.

population – the total number of certain beings living in one place.

protect – to guard someone or something from harm or danger.

reef – a line of underwater rocks, sand, or coral near the surface of the ocean.

risk – the possibility of danger, harm, or loss.

shallow – not deep.

zooplankton – tiny animals that live in oceans.